GW00992242

Dylan for the Cup

There was going to be a horse show in the village. Baz and Dylan were taking part in the jumping class.

Baz had made a jump in the field behind the farm, from two chairs and a wooden pole. She had been practising all day. But so far, it wasn't going very well. Every time Dylan tried the jump, he stopped short. Baz flew through the air and landed with a thump on the ground.

"Ouch! *Dylan*!" cried Baz, after the fifth time. "We're meant to go over *together*!"

Dylan stretched over the jump and licked her face.

Baz sighed.

"I'm going to see Jim," she said. "Maybe he can help."

3

Baz had spent all week with Dylan, leaving Scruffy and Molly on their own. Now Scruffy was bored – and when Scruffy was bored, there was sure to be mischief!

In the barn, the little Shetland bit on the bolt to his stable door and pulled it back. The door flew open. Then Scruffy trotted over to Molly, and opened her door, too.

Scruffy poked his head around the barn door.

Kath was in the house. Baz was at Jim's caravan. Wil had gone out – and left the farm gate open.

Nobody noticed as the ponies trotted out of the farm, down the lane towards the Big House.

At the Big House, Mrs Horace Morris was wearing her special garden hat to do the gardening.

"Such wonderful fun," she said.

As she pushed a large thistle into the ground, she didn't notice that two ponies on the other side of the hedge were watching her.

While Mrs Horace Morris's back was turned, Molly and Scruffy tugged at the tasty thistle. Then they hid behind the hedge again.

When Mrs Horace Morris turned back round, she was surprised to see the thistle had fallen over.

"Stand up when I'm talking to you!" said Mrs Horace Morris. She pushed the plant back into the ground.

Meanwhile, the ponies reached over the hedge again and ate a bit more thistle.

Mrs Horace Morris heard the chomping. Very slowly, she stopped digging and looked up.

"Ponies!" she screamed.

Wil heard her scream as he drove up the field.

Oh, no! he thought. *What's wrong now?*

"Go away! Shoo, ponies!" cried Mrs Horace Morris, as Wil got out of the Land Rover. She picked up a broom and waved it at Scruffy.

"Hold on, Mrs Morris," said Wil. "They're only ponies."

But Mrs Morris was very cross indeed.

"They're *eating* my plants!" she said.

And she waved the broom at Molly, with a sniff.

Down at the farm, Jim and Thomas watched while Baz and Dylan had another go at the jump.

"Ouch!" said Baz, as she landed on the floor again. "See, Jim? He always stops like that!"

Jim patted Dylan's neck.

"I'm sorry, Baz," he said. "It's not Dylan's fault."

Baz looked surprised.

"You mean it's *my* fault he won't jump?" she asked, puzzled.

Jim helped her get back onto Dylan.

"You have to *want* to jump, Baz," Jim told her. "You're holding Dylan back with the reins. He thinks you don't want to jump."

"But it's so high!" said Baz.

"Dylan can jump twice as high as that," Jim smiled. "Now off you go and try again."

U U U

Baz trotted off and turned towards the jump.

"Look *over* it, Baz!" cried Jim. "And let him go – he'll look after you!"

The jump got closer and closer.

When the jump was a few feet away, Baz gave Dylan a little kick and leaned forward.

"That's the way!" cried Jim, as Baz and Dylan sailed over the jump – together!

"Hooray!" cried Baz. "We did it, Dylan!"

A few days later, Kath was at Ambrose's shop when Mrs Horace Morris walked in.

She was looking for silver polish.

"I must clean the Horace Morris Cup," she said. "It's the prize for the children's jumping class at the horse show tomorrow."

"Baz is in that class!" said Kath.

Mrs Horace Morris gave a snooty smile.

"I don't think a thistle-stealing mountain pony will win the Horace Morris Cup!" she said nastily to Kath.

The next morning, Baz got up early and put on her riding clothes. Then she went down to the barn, to get Dylan ready, too.

But the stable was empty.

Baz ran back into the yard.

"Mum! Dad!" she cried. "Dylan and Scruffy are gone! They're missing! Oh, Mum! What am I going to do?"

Kath gave her a hug.

"Don't worry," she said. "They can't be that far away."

"Get into the Land Rover, everyone," Wil said. "We'll look in the fields. It's okay, Baz. We'll soon have Dylan back."

When the Land Rover hit a bump in the road, Baz gave a loud shout.

"Ouch! What am I sitting on?"cried Baz.

She pulled something off the seat of the car.

It was a thistle.

"A thistle?" said Wil. "That's it! Hang on, everyone. I think I know where they are!"

"Come on then, Dad!" cried Baz. "It's getting late!"

At the horse show, Mrs Horace Morris was standing in the tent for Very Important People. There were cups all around her, but the Horace Morris Cup was the biggest. She gave the cup a little polish with her handkerchief.

"Such a beautiful cup!" sighed Mrs Horace Morris. "I'm sure the child who wins you will live in a *very* big house."

Then Jim walked up to the tent.

"Excuse me, Mrs Morris," he asked. "Have you seen the Watkins family anywhere?"

Mrs Horace Morris looked surprised – and a little bit pleased.

"Why, no. I do hope Beatrice isn't late for her class," she fibbed.

Wil turned into Mrs Horace Morris's drive.

"If my hunch is right —" he said. "Yes!"

There were Dylan and Scruffy, happily eating the last of Mrs Horace Morris's thistles.

When they heard the Land Rover coming up the lane, the naughty ponies looked up.

"There they are!" shouted Baz.

She jumped out of the Land Rover and ran over towards them.

"You two!" she said, sternly.

"Come on, Baz. We'll have to take Scruffy in the trailer, too," said Wil. "There's not enough time to take him home."

Baz put her hand to her mouth.

"I'm going to miss my class!" she cried.

U   U   U

At the show, the children's jumping class was nearly over when the Watkins family drove onto the field.

"Quick!" Jim shouted. "You're only just in time!"

Mrs Horace Morris cleared her throat.

"Ladies and gentlemen," she said, "there were no clear rounds, so the winner of the Horace Morris Cup is —"

Someone pulled her sleeve.

"Yes, what is it?" she hissed.

"Hold on, Mrs Horace Morris. There's one more rider," said Jim. He pointed to Baz and Dylan.

Grumpily, Mrs Horace Morris picked up the microphone.

"And our final competitor is Beatrice Watkins, on Dylan," she said, crossly.

As Dylan trotted into the ring, Baz leaned forward and patted his neck.

"Okay, boy, it's just you and me now," she whispered.

She cantered towards the starting line.

Wil, Kath and Jim crossed their fingers as they watched Baz.

There were eight jumps. Dylan hopped over the first one, then jumped over the cross-poles and cantered round towards the gate.

"That's it, Baz!" cheered Jim and Thomas.

As Dylan skipped over each jump, the crowd clapped more and more loudly.

Just the last jump to go. Jim held his breath.

Dylan sailed right over it.

"This is – unnatural!" shouted Mrs Horace Morris.

"The winners!" shouted everyone else.

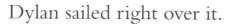

Baz and Dylan had cleared every single jump. They
were the winners of the Horace Morris Cup.

"Dylan! We did it!" cried Baz.

"And the winner of the Horace Morris Cup is – is – Beatrice Watkins on Dylan," croaked Mrs Morris.

"Oh, thank you!" cried Baz, as she took the cup.

Dylan decided to thank Mrs Horace Morris too.

He gave her a big, wet lick on her cheek.

"Oh my goodness! These creatures –" began Mrs Horace Morris.

Then Scruffy trotted forward.

"– are everywhere!" she cried.

And as Scruffy gave her a soggy pony "kiss" too, she sat down on the floor, with a bump!